KLAUS BAUMGART lives with his family in Berlin.
The LAURA'S STAR series has had multi-million sales
worldwide. It has been broadcast on TV throughout
Europe, including in the UK, and the first title, LAURA'S
STAR, has been made into a film. Klaus Baumgart was
the first German author/illustrator to be shortlisted for
the Children's Book Award in 1999 for LAURA'S STAR.

Also available by Klaus Baumgart:

Picture Books
LAURA'S STAR
LAURA'S CHRISTMAS STAR
LAURA'S SECRET
First Reader
LAURA'S STAR AND THE NEW TEACHER
LAURA'S STAR AND THE SLEEPOVER
Activity Book
LAURA'S STAR STICKER ACTIVITY BOOK

LITTLE TIGER PRESS
An imprint of Magi Publications
1 The Coda Centre, 189 Munster Road, London SW6 6AW
www.littletigerpress.com

First published in Great Britain 2006

HBK – ISBN-13: 978-1-84506-417-4 • ISBN-10: 1-84506-417-8
PBK – ISBN-13: 978-1-84506-418-1 • ISBN-10: 1-84506-418-6

Printed in China

2 4 6 8 10 9 7 5 3 1

Laura's Star

and the Search for Santa

Klaus Baumgart

English text by Fiona Waters

LITTLE TIGER PRESS
London

Christmas Biscuits

It was the last day of the school term and Laura couldn't wait for the Christmas holidays. Packed carefully in her school bag was the shiny red paper star she had made that day in class. Laura loved stars. She had her own amazing star that she had rescued once when it fell from the sky. It was her special friend and she told it all her secrets as it twinkled in the sky outside her bedroom window, or sometimes flew down to be with her!

As the final school bell rang, Laura raced home. She ran up the stairs and into the house, calling for her little brother.

"Tommy, Tommy! Where are you? I have something special to show you."

She went into his bedroom where Tommy was playing with his castle. He gazed at Laura as she pulled the red star triumphantly out of her bag.

"Look at this brilliant star I've made, Tommy. I shall put it on the tree in our holiday cottage as soon as we arrive. Won't it look lovely?"

But Tommy didn't answer.

"Tommy, you are going to help me decorate the tree, aren't you?" Laura asked anxiously.

Tommy shrugged. "I don't want to go away for Christmas," he said. "I want to stay here."

"But we will have great fun in the cottage. There will be lots of snow. We can have a snowball fight and build an enormous snowman," smiled Laura.

Tommy looked at his feet and mumbled something.

"What did you say, Tommy?" Laura asked.

"I said I don't want to go away for Christmas because Santa won't know where to find us," and Tommy looked so miserable that Laura knelt down beside him and gave him a big hug.

"Of course Santa will find us. He always knows where children are!"

"Are you sure?" he asked.

"Of course I'm sure. But I tell you what you can do to make extra sure," promised Laura. "You can write him a letter telling him where you will be!"

"Will that really work?" said Tommy hopefully.

"Yes, it will, but come on, we have something else to do first. What did Dad promise us today?" grinned Laura.

Tommy thought for a moment then beamed at Laura.

"Biscuits! Dad said we could make Christmas biscuits!"

"Then let's make them now, ready for Mum when she gets home from her concert," said Laura, and they dived into the kitchen.

Tommy fetched the baking trays and a bowl out of the cupboard, and Laura lined up the flour, the sugar and the other ingredients on the table. Dad appeared in the doorway. He was rushing about doing the packing for the trip to the cottage tomorrow.

"We are baking our Christmas biscuits now as a surprise for Mum," said Laura.

"What a good idea! I'm sure she'll be delighted. Let me know when you need me to put the oven on," said Dad.

Tommy kneaded the dough, and then Laura cut out the biscuits with the special cutters into star and moon shapes.

When Dad appeared again, they proudly showed him the trays filled with biscuits.

"Well done!" he said. "They look beautiful. I'll put them in the oven for you."

Laura whispered to Tommy. "Come on, while the biscuits are baking you can write your letter to Santa." So the two of them went into Tommy's bedroom.

It took quite a while to write the letter. Tommy carefully copied the address of the cottage and drew a little map. He was still worried that Santa wouldn't find them. Then a huge smile lit up his face.

"I know what! Let's tell Santa that we have baked some special biscuits and we will leave some out for him. He is sure to be hungry," he said happily.

They were just finishing the letter when Laura started sniffing.

"What is that funny smell? It smells like something burning."

"Oh no," yelled Tommy. "Our biscuits!"

Laura and Tommy dashed out of the bedroom and into the kitchen just in time to see Dad taking the baking tray out of the oven. The biscuits were completely black.

Tommy's eyes filled with tears. "The biscuits! I was going to leave some out for Santa. I wrote it in his letter! Now he definitely won't come to visit us!"

Dad picked him up in his arms.

"Of course Santa will come, Tommy, and we will have lots of biscuits for him. The shops are still open. We can go and buy him some special biscuits," he said cheerfully.

"Can we really, Dad?" Tommy hiccuped.

"Let's leave right now!" said Laura.

Too Many Santas

Laura and Tommy rushed to put on their hats, coats and shoes and then stood impatiently waiting for Dad to get ready.

"Come on, Dad!" shouted Tommy. "The shops will be shutting soon, and we must have the biscuits for Santa!"

Laura looked out of the window

and saw someone coming out of the house opposite. It was a large man with a bushy white beard wearing a red suit – Santa Claus!

"Tommy, quick! Look outside! It's Santa!" she said. The two children pressed against the window.

"Wow! Santa! Where is he going, Laura?" asked Tommy, wide-eyed.

Laura shrugged her shoulders. "I don't know, but we could follow him and find out!"

They ran to the front door, nearly tripping over Dad who was just putting on his shoes.

"Come on, Dad! Quick, we have to run after Santa," explained Tommy as he and Laura raced to the door and ran down the stairs.

"Wait for me," called Dad, but the children were already down the stairs and out on to the street. Sure enough, there was the man in the red suit just walking by the grocery shop.

"Perhaps he wants to buy carrots for the reindeer," whispered Tommy.

But Santa walked straight past the grocery shop. He walked a bit further down the street and into the large department store where Mum bought their clothes. Just as Tommy and Laura reached the entrance of the shop, Dad caught up with them.

"Please don't ever run away
like that again," he said, puffing for
breath. "You must stay close to me
when we are outside."

"But Dad, we are following
Santa," said Tommy excitedly.
"Look, there he is, coming
down the escalator."

At exactly the same
moment Laura cried,
"There he is, coming
down the street!"

Tommy turned
his head and
sure enough, there
was Santa walking
down the street
towards them. But he
was also coming down
the escalator, and just
then they saw *another*
Santa, across the
street by the
fire station.
"Three Santas?
There can't be
three Santas!"
cried Tommy,
completely
bewildered.

"Come on," said Dad quietly. "Let's go to the grocery store to buy Santa's special biscuits, and I will explain everything," and he took Tommy's hand in his big warm grasp.

"Santa is very, very busy at Christmas," Dad explained as they walked together. "While he's getting all the presents ready to deliver to children on Christmas Eve, his helpers make sure that the Christmas preparations in every town go just right. They dress like Santa, but they're not the *real* Santa."

They bought the biscuits and went home together. Tommy was very quiet and even Laura was feeling anxious. It had been so exciting to think they'd seen Santa. Surely he'd be able to find them in their holiday cottage . . . wouldn't he?

Laura needed to speak to her star. After dinner she hurried to her room and opened the window. Up above the rooftops the night was bright and clear, and there it was, her own special star.

"Oh, Star," she called quietly. "I'm so worried about Christmas. Tommy is very unhappy. He doesn't want to go to the cottage because he thinks Santa won't find us. What will we do if Santa forgets all about us?" And then the whole story poured out. The burned biscuits. Too many Santas on the street.

"Can you help me, Star? I really do want Tommy to look forward to Christmas properly."

Her star zig-zagged across the sky. For a moment it disappeared behind a cloud then reappeared again. It twinkled at Laura and then zig-zagged across the sky again. Laura thought hard and sighed.

How could they be sure that Santa would find them? Her star twinkled again and Laura suddenly realised what it was telling her.

"Maybe, rather than waiting for Santa to find us . . . we should find Santa!"

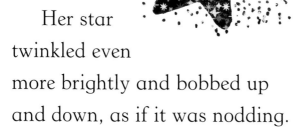

Her star twinkled even more brightly and bobbed up and down, as if it was nodding.

"Of course!" cried Laura. "That's it! Will you help me, Star?" she asked excitedly.

The sparkling star cartwheeled across the dark sky.

Laura smiled and said,
"Together we'll do it. We can show
Tommy that Santa knows exactly
where he is. I'm sure of it!"

Snow!

The next day was Christmas Eve, and the family were up early to set off for the holiday cottage. Mum woke Tommy and Laura with a big hug and the exciting news that it was snowing!

"I hope it snows more and more!" thought Laura as she pressed her nose against the

window. And it was coming down
quite heavily, the flakes sparkling in
the sun.

"Like little stars," thought
Laura happily, humming Christmas
carols as she finished packing her
things. But Tommy
was still anxious.
Laura just couldn't
get him to share her
excitement.

Eventually the car was loaded
and they all set off. Laura sat in the
back with Tommy as they drove
through the snowy streets.

Soon, they were out in the
countryside and all the trees were
covered in snow.

"You know, Tommy, this is just the sort of place where Santa might live," Laura whispered. "We should look out for him!"

Tommy's eyes lit up. "Really?" he said and, smiling, he sat up to peer out of the window at the snow.

"Just think, children," said Mum. "You will be able to build a huge snowman when we get to the cottage! And we can have a great big log fire and you can hang up your stockings for Santa."

"Can we put the special biscuits out for him too, even though we didn't make them?" said Tommy. Dad had told Mum about the burned biscuits.

"Of course we can!" said Mum. "I'm sure he will be very hungry by the time he reaches us."

"I think we are all going to be hungry by the time we get there," said Dad. "Look, the snow is getting deeper and deeper."

They all gazed out of the car window at the woods. The snow was falling heavily, and the world was sparkling white.

Mum and Dad looked at the map. In a whisper Tommy said to Laura, "Does Santa have a map for everyone's house?"

"I'm sure he does, Tommy," Laura said comfortingly. She could see he was getting worried again. It did seem to be taking a very long time to find the cottage.

They drove on, and then Dad said cheerfully, "Not far now! Look, this must be the turn-off," and they left the main road to go down a narrow, winding track

between the trees. Dad had to drive slower and slower through the snowdrifts until eventually he stopped the car.

"Oh dear!" he said. "I'm afraid the snow is too deep to drive any further. I think we're nearly there though. Let's see if we can go the rest of the way on foot."

Mum took hold of Laura's hand and Dad lifted Tommy on to his shoulders. Then they all set off through the icy woods.

At first it was fun wading
through the deep snow, but they
soon felt very tired.

Mum looked at Dad anxiously.

"I'm sure it can't be far now,"
he said with a cheery grin. "Let's
keep going."

It grew darker as they walked further into the woods and Laura began to feel anxious. What if they couldn't find the cottage? They were all getting rather cold and wet, and Tommy was looking really miserable again. Laura looked up at the sky. It would be wonderful if only her star was there.

Just then she caught sight of a silvery light above the trees – it was her star, come to help!

"Look over there!" she shouted. "I think I can see something."

"Where?" asked Mum.

"There, up ahead. There is a light, I am sure," said Laura.

Dad smiled happily. "I think you are right, Laura. Come on, everyone. We will soon be warm and dry again."

And so the family plodded on until

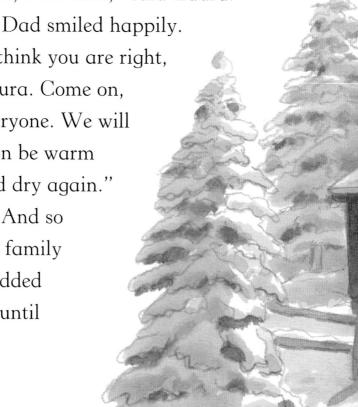

suddenly they saw a cosy-looking cottage just up ahead through the trees. Above it, Laura's star twinkled merrily. "Thank you," Laura whispered.

The Old Man

They all walked up the path to the cottage and Laura peeped through the window while Mum rang the doorbell. Light spilled on to the snow as an old man with a bushy white beard opened the door and looked out at the family.

"Well, well!" he laughed. "What have we here? Looks like four

snowmen to me. Come in, come in,
my dears. You must be frozen."

The family all tumbled gratefully
into the cheery warmth of the
cottage, stamping their feet to
get rid of the snow.

"You must be the family coming to stay for Christmas in the holiday cottage. I have been expecting to see you but I doubt you will get there tonight, the snow in the lanes is so deep. You are very welcome to stay here in my guest cottage."

Mum and Dad both started to speak at once.

"Oh no, we couldn't possibly . . ." said Dad.

"Oh that is so kind of you . . ." said Mum.

Everyone laughed, especially the old man. "I will take it that is a yes," he said, smiling, and he led them out through the snow to another pretty cottage.

But Tommy looked very miserable. "Santa definitely won't find us here," he whispered. "Laura, it's the wrong house."

"I shall put the kettle on for a hot drink while you get your bags from your car," said the old man to Mum and Dad. And turning to Laura and Tommy, he said, "I am sure you like hot chocolate, don't you?"

"Yes please, that would be lovely," said Laura, but Tommy hid behind her.

As the old man went off to boil the kettle, Tommy tugged Laura by the hand.

"We haven't got our Christmas tree or our decorations and we are not in the right house. Santa won't know we are here and anyway, I don't believe in him any more. This is going to be the worst Christmas ever!" and he burst into tears.

Laura gave him a big hug. "Shhh, Tommy. Please don't cry. I think it might all be wonderful actually! Doesn't the old man remind you of someone?"

Tommy shrugged.

"Someone very special," persisted Laura.

Tommy looked puzzled.

"Well, I think he looks a bit like Santa!" whispered Laura.

Tommy looked sideways at the old man as put wood on the stove. His eyes widened in excitement.

"Gosh, do you really think so?"
he asked.

Laura nodded her head, smiling.

Laura and Tommy sipped their
hot chocolate and soon Mum
and Dad came back,
staggering under

the weight of the suitcases and piles of exciting-looking parcels.

"Let's put these in a safe place so they will be ready for tomorrow morning," said Dad. "Come on, Tommy. You can help me with this big box."

"What a lovely cosy cottage this is," said Mum. "It's just right for our special Christmas adventure."

A Very Happy Christmas!

Laura and Tommy unpacked their things in the back bedroom of the cottage. The kind old man had brought them great steaming bowls of vegetable soup and big slices of delicious crusty bread and butter for supper. Then Mum had made them more creamy cups of hot chocolate and baked apples for dessert, while Dad arranged the presents by the fireplace ready for Christmas morning. Laura had already put her presents for Mum, Dad and Tommy there – she couldn't wait until morning!

Laura opened her suitcase and took out the red paper star she'd made at school.

"This will make it feel more like Christmas," she told Tommy. "I'll hang it up here on this beam."

But Tommy just curled up on his bed looking very forlorn.

"Christmas has all gone wrong!" he sniffed.

"Well, I think this cottage is a perfect place to spend Christmas," said Laura. "Even the woods are looking magical."

Tommy scrambled out of bed and padded across to the window. The snow was still falling thickly, sparkling in the moonlight – and starlight!

"Look, Tommy," cried Laura. "Look at the stars!" For there in the sky was her own special star.

It flew in a loop above the dark treetops and then dived down into the woods. 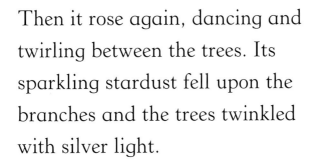 Then it rose again, dancing and twirling between the trees. Its sparkling stardust fell upon the branches and the trees twinkled with silver light.

"Thank you, dear Star," Laura whispered to herself.

When Tommy saw the sparkling trees, he gripped Laura's hand tightly. Silently, the two of them stood looking at the wonderland outside.

And then they noticed a figure, warmly wrapped up, walking across the snow. It was a man, with a sack over his shoulder.

"It's Santa!" said Tommy with a great cry of delight. "Laura, you were right! Oh, let's follow him now," he cried.

With trembling fingers, Laura and Tommy pulled on their boots and tiptoed towards the front door.

Laura reached up for their scarves and coats, hanging on pegs along the wall, and they crept out into the snow.

There was a shed next to the house and the door was ajar. Laura and Tommy slid through the shimmering snow and peeped round the door.

"Ooooohhhh!" gasped Tommy. For there inside the shed was a huge wooden sleigh.

"It must belong to Santa," he said in great delight. "We *have* found him, Laura! We *are* staying with Santa! Wow. This is going to be the best Christmas ever!"

Laura smiled at Tommy happily

and then looked up where her star, her very own special star, was twinkling over the shed.

"Santa must be just about to leave to deliver all the presents," she said. "Come on, let's get to bed or he won't be able to bring ours."

They raced back to the house and snuggled down into bed. Just before he fell asleep Tommy whispered, "No one will ever believe that we found Santa, Laura! It's wonderful!"

"Yes, it is," laughed Laura, taking one last look out of the window. There in the snow were sleigh tracks, leading out of the shed, into the woods. Santa had gone, off delivering his presents.

"Thank you, Star," she breathed. "Thank you so much for helping us find Santa."

And Laura and Tommy fell fast asleep, the light from her star twinkling through the window.

Other *Laura's Star* books

It's the new school year and Laura is very excited. But then she meets Joe West, who says her new teacher is really strict and gives loads of homework! Joe says that Mrs Williamson is the worst teacher in the whole school!

Suddenly Laura doesn't want to go back to school. In fact, she's dreading it. But maybe her special friend, the star, can help her out once more . . .

available in this series . . .

Laura and Sophie are very excited. They're going to have a sleepover at Sophie's aunt's house by the sea! They have great fun planning their weekend. They're going to collect shells, and have a midnight feast . . .

When Laura gets nervous about being away from home, her friend, the star, reassures her. But will the star help her when the sleepover doesn't quite go to plan?